## OXFORD
### UNIVERSITY PRESS

Great Clarendon Street, Oxford OX2 6DP

Oxford University Press is a department of the University of Oxford.
It furthers the University's objective of excellence in research, scholarship,
and education by publishing worldwide in

Oxford   New York

Auckland  Cape Town  Dar es Salaam  Hong kong  Karachi
Kuala Lumpur  Madrid  Melbourne  Mexico City  Nairobi
New Delhi  Shanghai  Taipei  Toronto
With offices in
Argentina  Austria  Brazil  Chile  Czech Republic  France  Greece
Guatemala  Hungary  Italy  Japan  Poland  Portugal  Singapore
South Korea  Switzerland  Thailand  Turkey  Ukraine  Vietnam

Oxford is a registered trade mark of Oxford University Press in the UK
and in certain other countries

Text © Gillian Lobel 2003
Illustrations © Helen Lanzrein 2003

The moral rights of the author and artist have been asserted

Database right Oxford University Press (maker)

First published 2003

British Library Cataloguing in Publication Data available

ISBN-13: 978-0-19-272561-5

ISBN-10: 0-19-272561-0

3  5  7  9  10  8  6  4

Typeset in Barbedor

Colour reproductions by Dot Gradations Ltd, UK

Printed in China by Imago

# Midnight Tiger

Written by
## Gillian Lobel

Illustrated by
## Helen Lanzrein

OXFORD
UNIVERSITY PRESS

Out in the dark, under the moon,
The midnight tiger prowls alone.

Soft through the jungle he pads along,
Then swishes his tail, and sings his song.

And all the creatures shiver and shake,
And crouch in their hollows wide awake.

And birds in their nests hide under their wings,
For none dare sleep when the tiger sings!

Then down to the shining midnight pool,
Where fishes swim in a silver shoal

The tiger steals –

And only the flare of his scarlet eye
Tells there's a tiger slinking by.

Quick is his paw as the lightning flash,
The water breaks like splintered glass,

But the tiger growls as his shining prey
Flick their tails and dart away.

Then through the flickering grass he glides,
And silent as a snake he slides

Into a glade of silver trees,
And watches in the gentle breeze

The midnight butterflies dance and play,
Green as grapes and bright as day.

A shadow shrieks in the glittering night,
And drifts like a ghost through the silver light

But she dare not face the blazing eye
Of the midnight tiger stalking by.

For he has a promise he must keep,
Before the stars drift home to sleep –

High on a rocky slope he springs,
Then lifts his head, and softly sings.

And there in the shadows
gleam golden eyes
Of a tigress who hears his lonely cries.

Together they sing till the moon goes down
And the stars are vanished
one by one.

Then the midnight tiger pads slowly home,
And into his head there comes a dream

Of warmth and food, and a place to sleep,
A few more steps

– a mighty leap –

And Tiger slides from the fading night,
Into a world of warmth and light.

'Look, Timmy's back!' the children cry,
And the midnight tiger breathes a sigh

And rolls on his back, while the children stroke
His downy fur, his stripy coat.

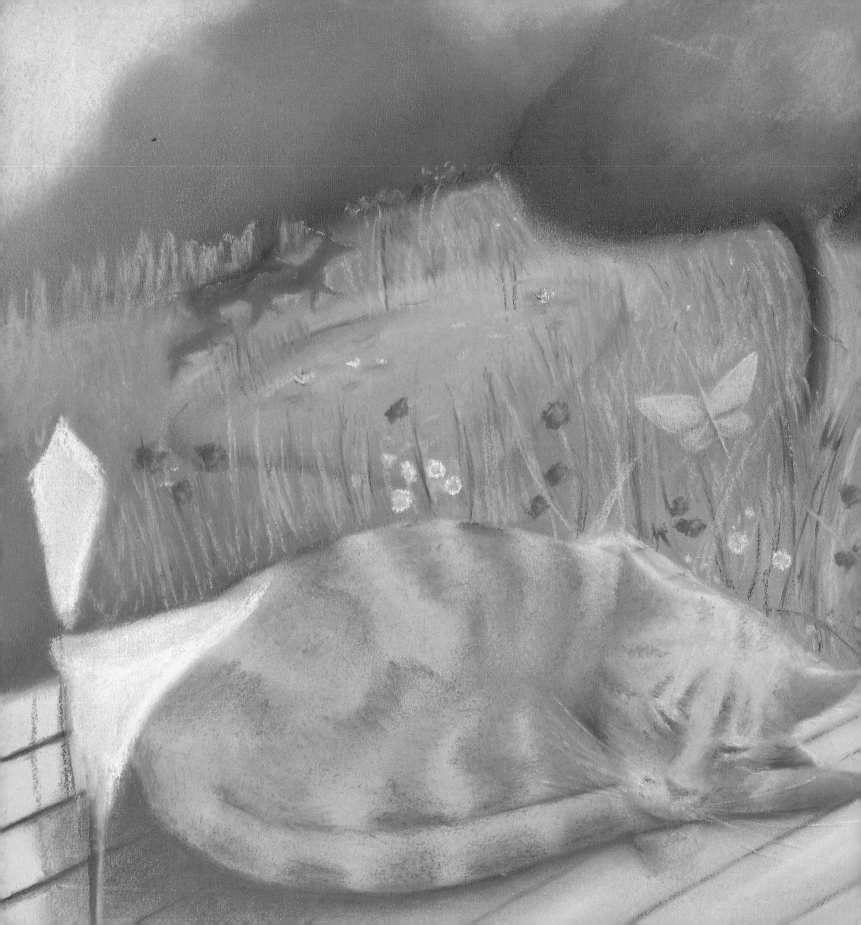

Then after a saucer of golden cream
He curls up tight to sleep – and dream

Of the midnight tiger who prowls alone
Out in the dark, under the moon.